MW01063810

The New Kitten

JOYCE CAROL OATES

Illustrated by Dave Mottram

HARPER

An Imprint of HarperCollinsPublishers

For Josephine, Anne, and Steve
—J.C.O.

To Sonya and Sara
—D.M.

The New Kitten

Text copyright © 2019 by The Ontario Review, Inc.

Illustrations copyright © 2019 by David Mottram

All rights reserved. Manufactured in China.

No part of this book may be used or reproduced in any manner whatsoever without
written permission except in the case of brief quotations embodied in critical articles
and reviews. For information address HarperCollins Children's Books, a division of
HarperCollins Publishers, 195 Broadway, New York, NY 10007.

www.harpercollinschildrens.com

Library of Congress Cataloging-in-Publication Data

Names: Oates, Joyce Carol, author. | Mottram, David, illustrator.
Title: The new kitten / by Joyce Carol Oates ; illustrated by David Mottram.
Description: First edition. | New York, NY : Harper, an imprint of HarperCollins
    Publishers, [2019] |
Summary: Cherie, a beloved cat, becomes very jealous when Cleopatra, a kitten, comes
    to live with her family.
Identifiers: LCCN 2018013451 | ISBN 9780062563927 (hardback)
Subjects: | CYAC: Behavior—Fiction. | Jealousy—Fiction. | Cats—Fiction. | Animals—
    Infancy—Fiction.
Classification: LCC PZ7.O1056 New 2019 | DDC [E]—dc23 LC record available at
https://lccn.loc.gov/2018013451

The artist used digital brushes created from scanned charcoal, pencil, and
watercolor drawings to create the illustrations for this book.
Book design by Alison Donalty • Lettering by Jenna Stempel-Lobell
19 20 21 22 23 SCP 10 9 8 7 6 5 4 3 2 1
❖ First Edition

Cherie was a fluffy gray adult kitty with a pink-tipped nose, white and black whiskers, four white boots, which she kept extra clean, and a PURR that was as loud as a motor. She was the only kitty in the Smith household, and she slept every night with little JoJo.

One day JoJo said, "We will be bringing home a surprise
for you, Cherie!"

Cherie thought, "I hope it is my favorite tuna treat."

Cherie had a little nest in a sunny upstairs window, where
she could watch birds and squirrels and switch her tail.

Cherie saw the Smith family return home. JoJo was carrying something that looked like a very small doll, except that it was moving.

Quickly Cherie ran downstairs. She was astonished to discover—what *was* it?

"Cherie, look! A new kitten has come to live with us. Her name is Cleopatra. Say hello, Cherie!"

Cleopatra blinked and mewed so softly you could almost not hear her. Her legs were very short and her tail was thin—not at all like Cherie's big, fluffy tail. She did not have soft, long, gray fur like Cherie but very short, smooth, shiny fur. She was so clumsy, she nearly fell over when she tried to walk.

JoJo had always fussed over Cherie. Now JoJo was making a fuss over the new kitten. That was *not* right.

Cleopatra tried to approach Cherie on her stubby legs to touch noses— but Cherie did not like this at all and HISSED.

Everyone was frowning at her, which Cherie had not ever seen before.
Cherie ran back into the house.

JoJo's friends could not wait to see the new kitten!
"Oh, how pretty Cleopatra is! Look at those leopard spots!"
They laughed at how she chased a little purple ball and how she rolled
over to show her spotted tummy. They laughed at how Cleopatra climbed
up onto her cat tree carrying a catnip mouse in her mouth.

"They used to say that I was pretty, too!" Cherie thought. "But now they don't care about me."

When JoJo called her for supper Cherie no longer came running
and PURRING.

At bedtime JoJo had to carry Cherie to her bed so that Cherie would sleep with her. In the middle of the night Cherie crept out of the room.

Cherie did not like the name "Cleopatra" at all.

Cherie did not like spots on a tummy.

Cherie did not like the cat tree because it had not been purchased for *her*.

Especially Cherie did not like how the new kitten put her paws in the water bowl to wash them—that was wrong. (You washed your paws with your tongue. That was correct.)

She was shocked that the new kitten played with her dry food as if it were some kind of beetle she had to leap and pounce on.

"If I spilled my food, I would be scolded," Cherie thought. Her tail swished and switched.

Though it was forbidden for Cherie to climb up onto the dining room table, this is exactly what Cleopatra did. From there she swatted at a mobile with cutout birds and brought it crashing down.

The Smiths only said, "Cleopatra is a kitten and doesn't know better." Everybody loved the *new kitten*. Cherie could not understand.

Next Cleopatra discovered how much fun it was to unwind rolls of toilet paper in the bathroom until the paper was all over the floor, torn and ragged.

Cherie hurried to find Mrs. Smith to bring her to see what Cleopatra had done.

Mrs. Smith laughed and took a picture.

Soon after, when no one was around, Cherie pulled the toilet paper out onto the floor. She tore and tore at it.

But Mr. Smith saw her and was not happy. "Cherie, bad cat! That is naughty."

Now all the bathroom doors were shut. It was clear; the Smiths no longer trusted *her*.

The new kitten was allowed to be naughty,
but Cherie was not.

Cherie could not nap any longer in her favorite places. No matter
where she went in the house, the new kitten followed her.

"Go away! *I don't like you*," Cherie HISSED.

The new kitten blinked. But after a while, she began following Cherie again.

It was especially upsetting to Cherie when the new kitten followed her to her favorite daytime place in the window.

One day Cherie found a new hiding place—she thought.

First, in the upstairs hall, you made sure that no one was watching—especially the new kitten.

Then you pulled open a door with your claws.

Then you climbed up the stairs into the attic—this was scary!

Cherie was happy because she believed the new kitten would *never find her.*

Suddenly Cherie was wakened by Cleopatra playing with her tail!

Cherie HISSED and jumped down. But Cleopatra was too small to jump down.

Cherie ran from the attic. She heard the new kitten mewing for help and thought, "Good!"

Cherie thought, "I will run away. They won't miss me!"

Cherie found a downstairs window that was open just enough for her to slip through.

She squeezed through a fence and went into the woods. She was very excited—there was so much to see and to smell!

A little white bunny rabbit hopped ahead of Cherie as if wanting to play.

But when Cherie followed the bunny, she saw him go into the ground down a hole that was too small for her.

"That was not very friendly," Cherie thought.

Next, little birds flew around her, cheeping. Cherie thought that they wanted to play, so she followed them deeper into the woods.

But the little birds kept ahead of her, high in the trees. They began to chatter—*Can't catch me! Can't catch me!*

"They are not very friendly," Cherie thought.

Now there were blue jays overhead. They screeched at Cherie and "buzzed" her by flying at her—*Go away! Go away! We don't like you.*

Cherie ran to hide in a hole in a tree. She was very upset.

Go away! Bad cat. I don't like you.

It was an owl! A big snowy-white owl that fluttered his wings and *hoo-hoo-hoo'd* at Cherie.

Cherie ran and ran!

But now she was beginning to worry that she could not find her way back home.

Suddenly she saw two little foxes rushing at her—*Hiss-hiss-hiss!* *We don't like you. Go away!*

Cherie did not understand why the foxes were so mean. Quickly she climbed a tree to escape them.

Cherie began to shiver. But there was a big moon in the sky, which helped her see the Smiths' house. It was not so far away.

"I wonder if they miss me," Cherie thought.

She thought of her tuna treats. She would be very happy to share them with the new kitten!

Cherie could hear a faint mewing. Was this Cleopatra? Cherie felt bad that she had left the new kitten on the rafter.

"She is just a kitten."

And so, now that the unfriendly foxes had gone away, Cherie climbed down from the tree and made her way back home.

Cherie hurried to the door and scratched and mewed.
"Why, Cherie! Where have you been?"

Cherie hurried to help Cleopatra down from the rafter, showing
her how to place her paws. Cherie did not shrink away when Cleopatra
touched noses with her to thank her.

Suppertime that evening was special, for JoJo gave both kitties
tuna treats. Cleopatra did not push her nose
into Cherie's bowl or try to play with
her tail.

Bedtime was even more special, for both kitties slept with JoJo,
who fell asleep listening to their PURRS.